Last copy

68 x 8/04 3/05   CL
75 x V08 4/08   (47) 7/97
77 x 11/09 1/10   (61) 3/02
84 x V 4/18   11/02

SAN DIEGO PUBLIC LIBRARY

CLAIREMONT

**ALWAYS BRING YOUR
CARD WITH YOU.**

Oct 1 1981

THE DAY I WAS BORN

THE DAY
I WAS BORN

by Marjorie and Mitchell Sharmat

illustrated by Diane Dawson

E. P. DUTTON   NEW YORK

Library of Congress Cataloging in Publication Data

Sharmat, Marjorie Weinman.   The day I was born.

Summary: Two brothers recall the day the younger was born.
[1. Birthdays—Fiction.   2. Brothers and sisters—Fiction]
I. Sharmat, Mitchell, joint author.   II. Dawson, Diane.
III. Title.
PZ7.S5299Day   1980   [E]   80-16313   ISBN: 0-525-28560-1

Published in the United States by E. P. Dutton, a Division
of Elsevier-Dutton Publishing Company, Inc., New York

Published simultaneously in Canada by Clarke,
Irwin & Company Limited, Toronto and Vancouver

Editor: Ann Durell   Designer: Claire Counihan

Printed in the U.S.A.   First Edition
10 9 8 7 6 5 4 3 2 1

for Andrew and his brother Craig
M.S. & M.S.

with thanks to Carol Bancroft
D.D.

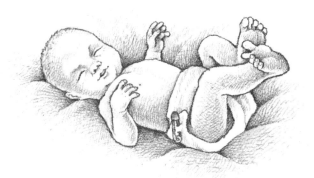

The day I was born, great events
were happening all over the world.

The day my brother was born, a traveling circus
in Bismarck, North Dakota, got a new chimp.

The day I was born, the president of the United States called from his office early in the morning. "Has Alexander come yet?" he asked.

The only call we got all day was from Grandma.
She doesn't sound a bit like the president,
and she doesn't have an office.

The day I was born, there was
a parade going to the hospital.

True. If you call my mother and father's
stalled car and three honking garbage trucks
behind it a parade. My mother had to get a ride
to the hospital in one of the garbage trucks.

The day I was born, the newspapers wanted
to take my picture and put it on the front
page. But my father was afraid of germs.

They had to settle for a picture
of the garbage man and his truck.

The day I was born, they tried to pick the
best name ever. My mother and father liked
Hiram, which means noble, and Grandma and
Grandpa wanted Aylmer, which means noble *and*
famous. My brother kept nagging for Alexander,
as in Alexander the Great, and he won.

That was the day Renaldo up the street
had five puppies. I helped name them.
I had three names left over.
But my mother and father didn't like
Slugger or Grits.

The day I was born, my mother and father said I was bright and adorable.

Slobber, slobber, slobber.
Kitchy-kitchy-coo.

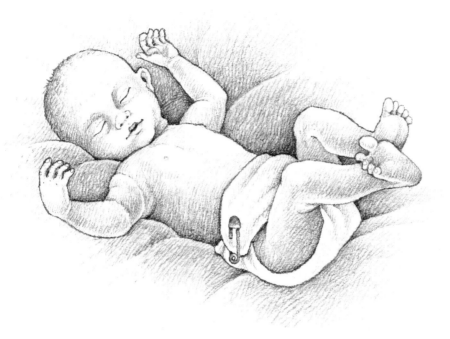

And handsome.

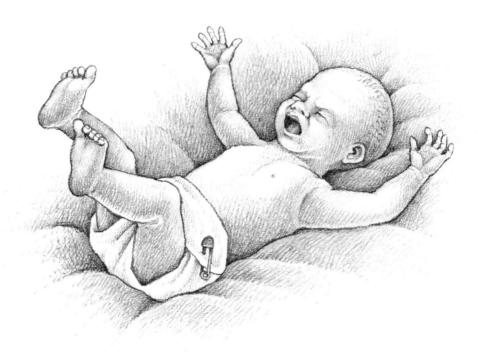

Ha! All gums. No teeth. Little chimp.

The day I was born, my father
went to a toy store and bought me
some colored fish on strings,
some rings,
a bar to pull on,
and a fire truck.

Guess who got the fire truck?

The day I was born, twenty-eight people
went out and bought cards.

There were only eighteen cards, and one of those didn't count. It was from Mrs. Dinglehoff, who even sent a get-well-soon card when our tomatoes got the blight.

The day I was born, my father
took my brother to a restaurant
to celebrate.

It was either that or reheated creamed
cauliflower, because nobody had time
to fix anything else.

The day I was born, I got a headache.
My brother kept yelling, "Send him back!"

So what? I didn't like
my turtle right away, either.

I was born six years ago today.
On that day, I got two parents and
a brother. My brother drew a picture
of himself and gave it to me.

In the last six years, I got
to like my turtle a lot. But I
like Alexander even better.

"Happy Birthday, Alexander.
I hope you still like garbage trucks."